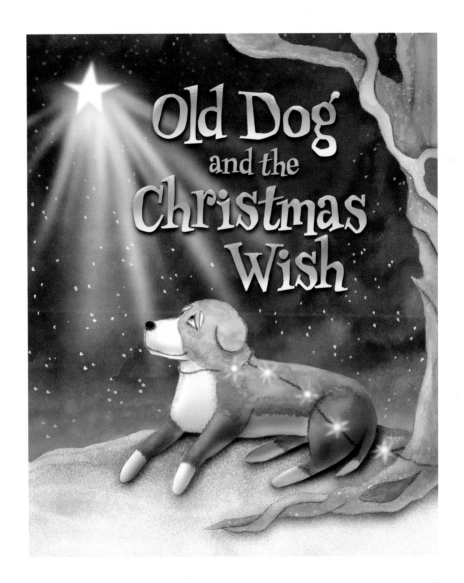

Old Dog
and the
Christmas
Wish

Written and illustrated
by Christine Davis

Old Dog and the Christmas Wish

Printed in China

Lighthearted Press Inc.
P.O. Box 90125
Portland, OR 97290

ISBN-13:   978-0-9659225-3-1
ISBN-10:   0-9659225-3-7

10 9 8 7 6 5 4 3 2 1

A heartfelt thank you...

To Sarah Fine and her magical designer's touch...
for building a bridge between my painted pages
and the visions that danced in my heart

To Grace Henson... for picking up her pencil and
helping me find my lost dog

To my sister, Aeylin... for her editorial expertise

To Maya, the dog I met at Christmas in 2004...
for letting me into her life so we could break her
loose from her chains – may she run free for many
happy years

For Jake,
the four-legged
love of my life

You are the heart
and spirit
of this book

May you never
stop watching
over me

The old dog stood at the end of the broken-down fence.
The chain around his neck stretched just far enough for him to
see into the neighbor's yard. A wreath hung on their door, and
Christmas lights had been strung around the windows.
Boxes of decorations waited to be opened.

The dog walked stiffly back along his chain and crawled under a fallen tree. An angel perched on the fence watching him. She saw the sadness in his tired eyes and knew his time was coming to an end. The angel looked to the heavens and asked if the old dog might know the magic of Christmas just once before he left the earth.

It was the sparkling lights that woke up the dog. They twirled around the fallen tree and twinkled down his chain. A shining star danced above his head. Two bowls lay before him, and he took the food and water gratefully. When he was done, he lifted his gray muzzle upward. There by the fence he saw her. Slowly his matted tail began to wag.

Then he put his head on his paws and drifted off to sleep. The bowls disappeared and the twinkling lights faded away. But the dancing star shone down upon the sleeping dog throughout the night.

The next day was Christmas Eve.
Visitors came and went from the neighbor's home.
It was evening before the dog walked to the end of
the fence and looked around the corner. Wooden
figures now stood in the grass. Two knelt over a
baby sleeping in a bed of hay. A cow and a donkey
huddled nearby. A shepherd stood with his sheep.
Above them, a glorious star illuminated the heavens.

The old dog looked at the sleeping baby and knew this child was special. He searched the yard, certain there would be a dog at this wondrous celebration to keep watch over the child. But no dog stood with the animals. No dog sat by the child in the hay.

Something awakens in the heart of a dog when
he knows that he is needed. This dog felt his place was at
the baby's side, keeping watch over the sleeping child. He
pulled hard against his chain, but it wouldn't break free.

He pulled again, but there was no strength left
in his weary body. A bitter wind was beginning to blow.
He pulled one last time, but his tired legs gave out.
The old dog sank to the ground.

The dog looked up and saw the brilliant star blazing in the night sky. Beams of light were falling to the earth around him. A hand reached down from the heavens and stroked his head. "Good and faithful friend." They were the last words he heard as he closed his eyes.

The angel went to the

old dog's side and whispered words
of comfort into his stilled heart.

There came on the wind a sound from the neighbor's yard, whisperings of a Christmas wish. The angel's wings fluttered with joy, for the wooden figures were beginning to stir! The cow and the donkey pawed the ground as their breath hung like clouds in the frigid air.

Wind brushed the folds of the shepherd's cloak. The kneeling figures were praying softly. And the child…the little baby…opened his eyes and reached out his tiny hands in welcome toward the dog.

The paws twitched. The legs moved. His body arched along the mud-covered ground. Then the dog began to breathe. With every sacred breath, the beat of his pure and loving heart was growing stronger. He opened his eyes and lifted up his head.

The old dog came lightly to his feet. The chain had fallen from his neck, and the matted fur had disappeared. A white light surrounded his beautiful coat, and a star blazed from the end of his magnificent tail!

He looked back at the fallen tree
and the place that had been his home.
Then he came to the angel who had seen
his true heart. She held him one last time.
The shining tail wagged excitedly.

The dog jumped over the broken chain and ran around the fence. He trotted up to the bed of straw and stood before the child. The star-tipped tail wagged with happiness. He saw that all was well and as it should be. And the baby welcomed the old dog home.

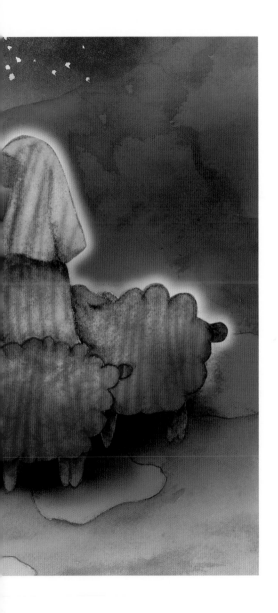

Then the dog turned around once...twice... three times and took his place by the child's side. The baby closed his eyes. The animals became silent. The wooden figures went still.

On Christmas morning, the neighbors
came outside to greet their guests. No one noticed
the wooden dog sitting beside the child. Above
them, the angel smiled as she disappeared into the
Christmas sky.

And somewhere in the mists of forever,
a baby sleeps on a bed of straw. His adoring parents
kneel beside him as angels sing of the newborn's birth.
Wise men come bearing great gifts. A shepherd gazes
in wonder while the animals quietly eat their hay. And
there, by the side of the sleeping child, sits a dog with a
star at the end of his tail keeping watch over them all.